DON'T
GET
CAUGHT

IN THE GIRLS
LOCKER ROOM

Other books by Todd Strasser

Don't Get Caught Wearing the Lunch Lady's Hairnet

Help! I'm Trapped in a Supermodel's Body

Don't Get Caught Driving the School Bus

Help! I'm Trapped in a Vampire's Body

Y2K-9: The Dog Who Saved the World

Help! I'm Trapped in a Professional Wrestler's Body

Help! I'm Trapped in My Lunch Lady's Body

Help! I'm Trapped in a Movie Star's Body

Help! I'm Trapped in My Principal's Body

Help! I'm Trapped in My Camp Counselor's Body

Help! I'm Trapped in an Alien's Body

Help! I'm Trapped in Obedience School Again

Help! I'm Trapped in Santa's Body

Help! I'm Trapped in the First Day of Summer Camp

Camp Run-a-Muck series:

#1: Greasy Grimy Gopher Guts

#2: Mutilated Monkey Meat

#3: Chopped Up Little Birdy's Feet

Help! I'm Trapped in My Sister's Body

Help! I'm Trapped in the President's Body

Help! I'm Trapped in My Gym Teacher's Body

Help! I'm Trapped in Obedience School

Help! I'm Trapped in the First Day of School

Help! I'm Trapped in My Teacher's Body

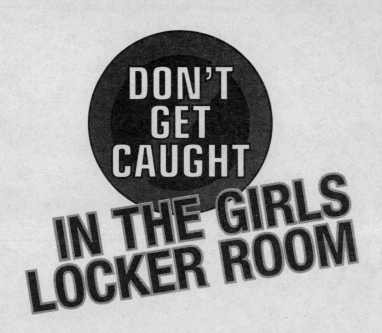

DON'T GET CAUGHT IN THE GIRLS LOCKER ROOM

TODD STRASSER

AN
APPLE
PAPERBACK

SCHOLASTIC INC.

New York   Toronto   London   Auckland   Sydney
Mexico City   New Delhi   Hong Kong

ISBN 0-439-21064-X

12 11 10 9 8 7 6 5 4 3   1 2 3 4 5 6/0

Printed in the U.S.A.   40

First Scholastic printing, March 2001

To Katie and Ryan

DON'T GET CAUGHT
IN THE GIRLS
LOCKER ROOM

"**W**ould someone like to tell me why we had to sneak into school early this morning?" my friend Wilson Kriss asked with a yawn.

School wouldn't begin for another twenty minutes. Wilson, Dusty Lane, and I were the only people in the hallway.

"To see the future of in-school transportation," Dusty announced. He pulled a blue plastic chair with metal legs out of a classroom. We were standing at the end of the long, empty hall. During the night Sam the custodian must have polished the floor because the tiles glistened.

"I hate to tell you this," I said, "but chairs are for sitting, *not* moving."

"Behold." Dusty pressed a button on his wristwatch. Then he started to run down the shiny hallway pushing the chair in front of him. About a third of the way down the hall, he jumped into the chair. The next thing Wilson and I knew,

Dusty was sitting in the chair, holding tight as he sailed over the polished tiles.

"Admit it, Wilson," I said. "That looks like fun."

"There's just one problem," Wilson replied.

"What?"

"In about a second Dusty's going to slide right past the office."

"So?" I said.

"They get into school early, too."

S till sitting in the chair, Dusty slid past the office. A second later the office door started to open.

Wilson and I dove around a corner so we wouldn't be seen. Down the hall, Principal Chump, AKA Monkey Breath, came out.

"What's going on?" Wilson whispered as I peeked around the corner.

"Monkey Breath is standing in the hall scratching his head," I whispered back.

"Where's Dusty?"

"Gone."

"You think Monkey Breath saw him?" Wilson asked.

"From the way he's scratching his head I get the feeling he isn't sure *what* he saw."

Down the hall our principal shook his head and went back into the office. A few moments later Wilson and I heard a light scraping sound. We swiveled around. Sliding down the hall behind us was Dusty.

And he was still sitting in the chair!

"Ta-da!" Dusty hopped out of the chair and pressed a button on his watch. "Forty-seven seconds!"

"You went *all the way* around the school?" I gasped.

"Sure did."

"No way!" Wilson argued. "You can't turn corners in a chair."

"When you get to a corner you jump off and take another running start," Dusty explained. "But *most* of the time you're in the chair."

"You know how close you came to getting busted by Monkey Breath?" I asked.

Dusty's jaw fell. "Serious?"

"He came out of the office just after you passed," said Wilson. "But by then you were gone."

Dusty grinned. "Should make it interesting tomorrow."

"What are you talking about?" Wilson asked.

Dusty pointed at his watch. "Tell me one of you guys isn't going to *try* to break the world long distance chair sliding record?"

Wilson and I traded a look.

"He's got a point," I said.

Wilson nodded. "Looks like we'll be back here early tomorrow."

3

My friends and I are really different. Dusty's tall, thin, and easygoing. Wilson's short and a bit pudgy. He's a worrier. And except for the fact that a lot of girls say they have crushes on me, I think I'm pretty average. The one thing we have in common is getting away with as much stuff as possible. It's natural to feel that way at the Hart Marks Middle School, where there are about six trillion rules against everything.

But, as far as we knew, no rule against chair sliding.

Dusty put the chair back in the classroom. It was time to join the crowd of kids outside waiting for the morning bell to ring.

"You hear about Rachel Smath's party?" Wilson asked as we snuck out the door at the back of the boys locker room. "Her parents won't be there. Know what that means?"

"We can wreck the place?" Dusty guessed hopefully.

"No, they'll want to play spin the bottle," Wilson said.

"Then there's no way I'm going," I said.

"Me, neither," said Dusty as we walked across the dew-covered grass.

"What is it with girls and kissing?" Wilson asked.

"Don't ask me," I said.

"Know what I heard?" Dusty said. "Sometimes girls kiss each other. Like, for practice."

"Gross!" Wilson made a face.

"Hey, better they kiss each other than kiss us," I said.

"You're right," Wilson said. "We're never, *ever* gonna kiss girls, right?"

"Right," I said.

"Right," said Dusty.

"So there's no way we're going to that spin the bottle party," Wilson concluded as we reached the bus circle, where buses were dropping off kids.

"I'm surprised there are any bottles left considering how psyched Alice is about that stupid recycling competition," I said.

"Talk about Alice." Dusty nodded toward the bus circle. Wearing a bright green recycling cap, Alice Appleford was greeting each busload of kids.

"We better hide before she sees us," I said, quickly turning away.

"Too late," said Dusty.

Alice was headed in our direction.

Alice Appleford is blond and works hard to be the world's most excellent kiss-up. As she came toward us, she gave me that gooey smile that always made me want to run away as fast as I could.

Briiiinnnggg! Just then the morning bell rang and kids started to go in.

"Kyle, could I talk to you for a second?" Alice asked.

"Sorry, Alice, I really have to get into school." I tried to go around her.

She stepped in front of me, blocking my path. "It'll only take a second."

"Have fun, Kyle." Dusty winked as he and Wilson went up the walk toward the upper-grade entrance.

I turned to Alice. "So what's up?"

"I'll get right to the point, Kyle," Alice said. "I need a new coanchor on the morning news show."

Every morning the school TV station, Hart TV, had a five-minute news show. We used to call it the *Gary and Alice Show*, because this eighth-grade jerk Gary Gordon was Alice's coanchor. But then Gary got nailed on video saying really bad (but true) stuff about Alice and she gave him the boot. Now the cohost position was open.

"You'd be perfect, Kyle," Alice said. "You're charming and good-looking and all the girls love you. It would be great for our ratings."

"Let me think about it," I said.

Alice frowned and put her hands on her hips. "That's what you *always* say. I asked if you'd help with the recycling competition and you said you'd think about it. I ask if you'd be my coanchor and you say you'll think about it. But you *never* do!"

"This time I promise I . . . er . . ." I glanced over my shoulder at school. "Hey, don't you have to go on TV pretty soon?"

Alice checked her watch. "Yes." But instead of leaving, she looked up at me and her eyes had a sweet, gooey cast. "Did you hear about Rachel's party?"

I swallowed hard. "Party? Uh . . . I'm not sure."

"Her parents won't be there." Alice gave me a searching gaze. "Know what that means?"

"That they'll be someplace else?"

"No, silly," she said. "It means we'll be able to do anything we want."

"Like play charades?"

Alice rolled her eyes. "Don't play dumb, Kyle. You know *exactly* what I mean."

Alice hurried into school so she wouldn't be late for her TV show. Meanwhile, I felt a shiver of dread. Alice had just made it clear that she hoped I'd go to Rachel's party and play spin the bottle. The thought was enough to make me want to barf for a week.

I got to homeroom just as Hart TV went on and Alice began the morning show alone. Not a single kid in class was paying attention. Dusty sits next to me in homeroom. He leaned over. "What'd she want?"

"She wants me to be her coanchor," I said. "She says it'll be good for the ratings."

"What ratings?" Dusty asked. "We only have one TV show. It's not like anyone has a choice."

On the homeroom TV Alice was talking about her favorite topic, the recycling competition. "Remember, everyone, if we win this competition, the whole school gets to go to Big Splash Water Park. But it's not going to be easy. My spies tell me that over at Burt Ipchupt Middle School in Jeffersonville they've collected just as many bottles and cans as we have."

"Spies?" Dusty repeated in disbelief.

Suddenly, on the TV a hand reached in and handed Alice a sheet of paper. Alice looked a little flustered as she quickly read it and faced the camera again.

"Uh, I've just been informed by Principal Chump that there will be an emergency upper-school assembly. All sixth-, seventh-, and eighth-grade homerooms are to go to the auditorium immediately."

The TV went dark. Our homeroom teacher, Ms. Taylor, looked up and frowned. "Anyone know what this is about?"

Everyone in class shook their heads. We'd never heard of an emergency assembly before.

As the mobs of sixth, seventh, and eighth graders crowded through the auditorium doors, the evil Dr. Monkey Breath stood on the stage. Monkey Breath is a small man with dark hair and big ears. Normally, he's neatly dressed in a dark suit. But today his suit looked wrinkled and his hair was a mess.

He waved his arms and yelled into the microphone: "Take your seats quickly. Hurry! We don't want this to cut into your class time."

"Actually, we do," Dusty whispered as he and I went down the aisle looking for seats.

"Hey, guys." Alice Appleford and Rachel Smath were sitting in a row with a couple of extra seats. You could tell from the tone of Alice's voice that she wanted us to sit with them. Rachel is a cute girl with red hair and an upturned nose. She is part of Alice's supercompetitive goody-goody kiss-up crowd, and she was giving Dusty the same kind of gooey, dreamy look that Alice often gave me.

"Hey, girls." We waved back, then pretended we were being swept past their row by the crowd of kids behind us.

If Alice and Rachel were in the back, Dusty and I wanted to be near the front. Meanwhile, sitting in chairs onstage behind Monkey Breath were Samantha Mopp, the janitor; Ms. Ivana Fortune, our assistant principal; Mr. Gutsy, the boys' gym teacher; and Ms. Step, the girls' gym teacher.

Ms. Fortune is the world's only babe assistant principal. She has red hair and red lips and wears tight dresses and high heels. Mr. Gutsy is tall and skinny and bald and always has a smile on his face. Up onstage they spent more time looking at each other than at the crowd.

"A weird collection of people," Dusty commented.

"I was thinking the same thing," I said. "What do you think this is about?"

As if Monkey Breath had heard me, he put his hand over the mike and wagged his finger at Dusty and me. "You two, over here."

Dusty and I went to the edge of the stage. Monkey Breath kneeled down. Not only was his suit rumpled and his hair a mess, but his right eye was twitching. "Strange thing happened this morning, boys. I was standing in the office before school started and out of the corner of my eye I thought I saw a kid who looked just like Dusty slide past in a chair."

"That *does* sound weird," I agreed.

"Think you imagined it?" asked Dusty.

"That's the problem," answered Monkey Breath. "Maybe I did. That's why I want to know if it's possible."

"I guess it's possible," Dusty said.

Monkey Breath blinked. "You're admitting it?"

Dusty shook his head. "No, but — "

"No buts," said Monkey Breath.

"Huh?"

"I said. 'No buts'," our principal repeated. "The answer is either yes or no, but no buts."

"Well, I was just going to say that it's probably *possible* to slide down the hall in a chair," Dusty explained.

Monkey Breath nodded. "I know that. Was it you?"

"If it was, why would he tell you?" I asked.

"Because if you get caught doing something wrong, you should admit it," said our principal.

"He didn't get caught," I pointed out.

"So if you *don't* get caught you *shouldn't* admit it?" Dusty asked.

"No," answered Monkey Breath. "You should admit it whether you get caught or not."

"What if you didn't do it?" I asked.

"If you didn't do it, you shouldn't admit it," replied Monkey Breath.

"We shouldn't admit we didn't do it?" Dusty sounded confused.

"No. You *should* admit it if you didn't do it," said Monkey Breath.

"Wait a minute," I said. "I don't get this. If we did it, we should admit it, but if we didn't do it, we should *also* admit it?"

Monkey Breath frowned and his right eye started twitching even faster. "That doesn't sound right. It must be those little green women."

"What little green women?" Dusty asked.

Monkey Breath didn't seem to hear him. By now the auditorium was filled with noisy, clamoring kids wondering what this "emergency assembly" was all about.

"Listen, Principal Chump," I said, "we can continue this conversation later. Right now you better get this crowd under control."

Monkey Breath stood up and went back to the microphone. "Quiet, everyone!" he shouted. "Take your seats and quiet down."

Dusty and I turned away and looked for seats.

"Little green women?" Dusty whispered.

All I could do was shrug.

"Yo, dudes!" Wilson waved and pointed at some seats he was saving. As we squeezed into his row and sat down, Monkey Breath started the assembly: "All right, everybody. I'll make this simple. At lunch yesterday Ms. Mopp's key ring broke in the cafeteria. Her keys fell to the floor and a number of you were kind enough to help her pick them up. Ms. Mopp thought she had all the keys, but it now appears that one key is still missing. Unfortunately, it is the master key to all the lockers in the boys and girls locker rooms."

"Ooooooooohhhhh!" "Yeeeeeeaaaahhhhhhh!" The audience cheered and applauded. Up on the stage, Sam the custodian and some of the others frowned, but Ms. Fortune and Mr. Gutsy smiled warmly at each other as if they were completely unaware of what was going on.

"What master key?" Dusty whispered. "They all have combinations."

"No, there is a master key," Wilson whispered back. "Next time you're in the locker room look under the lock dial. You'll see a keyhole."

"So the gym teachers can get into a locker even if they don't know the combination?" I guessed.

"Exactly," said Wilson.

The crowd in the auditorium was still hooting and hollering.

"Quiet! Quiet!" Monkey Breath shouted from the stage. "We are not sure whether the key is still lost, or whether someone took it on purpose. The problem is that if we do not get the key back, we will have to replace all the locks on all the lockers in both locker rooms. This will be ex-tremely expensive and may result in the cancellation of our annual overnight camping trip to Squeegee Lake."

Monkey Breath was always threatening to take things away from us for financial reasons. The annual campout at Squeegee Lake was the bomb because the lake was full of frogs and snakes and other good stuff to gross out girls with.

"Yesterday after school, we searched the cafeteria very carefully," Monkey Breath went on. "But we were unable to find the key. This leads us to believe that someone has it. Needless to say, if one of you does have that key, we expect you to return it. The easiest way is to put it in an envelope and leave it on any teacher's desk."

Wilson leaned toward Dusty and me. "Guys, be on the lookout for an envelope on a teacher's desk. It'll probably have the master key in it."

He said it loud enough for the whole row to hear. Everyone laughed. Even our homeroom teacher, Ms. Taylor, grinned.

"I will wait a few days to see if the master key is returned," Principal Chump said. "If it isn't, you may very well lose your camping trip. That's all. You should now go to your second-period class."

With all the confusion over the emergency assembly, my friends and I knew we'd have time to mess around and still not get marked late for our next class. We just had to find a place where a teacher was unlikely to catch us.

"You guys going to the boys' room?" asked Cheech the Leech. Cheech is this kid who follows the cool kids and imitates whatever they do. Actually, there are probably a lot of kids who do that, but somehow Cheech is a hundred times more obvious than anyone else.

"What do you think?" Wilson asked.

"I think it's the place to be," said Cheech.

Cheech followed us into the boys' room. He went up to the metal mirror and started fixing his hair.

"Yo, Cheech, lookin' hot." Dusty grinned.

"What's the occasion?" I asked.

"Rachel Smath's party, dudes," Cheech said.

"Right," Dusty said. "The big spin the bottle bash. There's just one thing I don't understand."

"What?" said Cheech.

"You don't really *want* to kiss girls, do you?"

Cheech smiled. "Don't knock it till you've tried it, dudes."

"Maybe the real question is, what girl wants to kiss Cheech?" I joked.

Cheech kept right on smiling. "A lot more than will ever want to kiss *you*, Kyle."

"Ooooh!" Dusty and Wilson grinned. "You gonna take that, Kyle?"

It was tempting to get into a serious cut-down war with Cheech, but I couldn't see the point of it. "Forget it, guys, this is dumb. Let's go."

As we started out of the boys' room, Wilson turned to Cheech. "Just for your information, dude, every girl in this school thinks Kyle is the numero uno studly hunk. You'd have to be wacko to think they'd rather kiss you than him."

"We'll see about that," Cheech replied mysteriously.

Out in the hall we headed for our next class.

"I can't believe you let him get away with that, Kyle," Wilson muttered.

"Get away with what?" I asked.

"Saying girls would rather kiss him than you."

"Tell you the truth," I said, "I hope he's right."

At lunch I joined Dusty and Wilson at our regular table.

"Nice to be able to sit where we want again," I said as I set my tray down.

"You have to hand it to Wilson," Dusty said. "He said he'd send the Lunch Monitors from H.E.L.L. back to where they came from, and he did."

"We go where no rule has gone before," Wilson chanted our motto and the three of us slapped hands. A month before, Monkey Breath had hired the Lunch Monitors from H.E.L.L. to bring order to the cafeteria. They'd even tried to assign us seats at lunch tables. Wilson was the leader of the rebellion. Two weeks later, the monitors were gone and once again we were sitting where we pleased.

Our pal Melody Autumn Sunshine usually sits at the table next to ours. Melody has long braided brown hair and she's supersmart. She smiled at me. "Hi, handsome."

She always says that and it always makes me blush. I can't figure out whether she does it just to tease me or whether it means something more serious.

"What do you think about this master key stuff?" she asked. "Think someone really has it?"

"Why would anyone want that key?" Dusty said. "Does anyone really keep anything valuable in their gym locker?"

"Dirty socks," I said.

"Smelly T-shirts," said Wilson.

"What if a girl has the key?" Melody asked.

"Is there anything in a guy's locker she'd want?" Wilson asked.

"Extremely doubtful," said Melody. "Besides, what girl is going to risk getting caught in the boys locker room?"

"Right," I said. "And what guy would risk getting caught in the girls locker room?"

"It's just not worth it," said Dusty.

"Unless . . ." Melody started to say.

"Unless what?" Wilson asked.

"Unless," said Melody, "he wanted to read the kissing book."

"The what?" I said.

"It's this rumor," Melody explained. "That there's supposed to be a book that rates how every boy in school kisses."

"What's that got to do with the girls locker room?" Wilson asked.

"They say that's where it's hidden," Melody said. "In an empty locker. Some of the girls know the combination."

"Wait a minute," Wilson said. "How would they get the information on how guys kiss?"

"From playing spin the bottle," Melody said. "Plus whatever extracircular kissing goes on."

"Extracircular kissing?" Wilson repeated with a frown.

"Like when it's not at a spin the bottle party," Melody explained.

"Oh." Wilson nodded. "Well, that's nothing Dusty, Kyle, and I would ever have to worry about, right guys?"

Neither Dusty nor I answered.

"Have *you* ever seen this book?" Dusty asked Melody.

She shook her head. "It's probably just a joke someone made up."

"I *hope* so," I said, then instantly wished I'd kept my mouth shut. Too late. Wilson frowned at me.

"Why?" he asked.

"Why what?" I tried to act dumb.

"Why do you hope it's only a joke?"

"Uh . . . because it could be really embarrassing," I said. "I mean, what guy wants to be rated on his kissing ability?"

"Right." Wilson caught on. "Because that would mean you'd actually *kissed* a girl."

"It could be like baseball," added Dusty. "One day you're hitting home runs, the next day you're striking out. What if you have a bad day, and *that's* the day they write about? Next thing you know, your stats are way down and Alice is doing the daily kissing report on TV every morning."

"At least that would get people to watch her show," Wilson said.

The thought made me wince.

"You guys seem awful worried about something that probably doesn't even exist," Melody pointed out.

Dusty and I shared a surprised look, and then we both quickly shook our heads.

"Hey, I'm not worried," Dusty said.

"Me, neither," I added.

"Funny, you both look pretty worried to me," someone said. We looked up. It was Gary Gordon, Alice's former TV coanchor, and the most conceited double rump scrubbing butt ox in the eighth grade.

Gary couldn't stand us and we couldn't stand him. The only reason he'd come over was to talk to Melody, who he had a crush on.

"You going to Rachel's party?" he asked her.

"Why, Gary?" Dusty asked teasingly. "You think she'll play spin the bottle with you?"

"You guys are so immature," Gary scoffed.

"Oh, yeah, and you're Mr. Maturity," Wilson replied with a chuckle.

"At least I know what to do with a girl if I'm alone with her," Gary bragged.

"I bet that's not what the book says," Dusty said.

Gary frowned. "What book?"

"*You* don't know about the kissing book?" Dusty taunted him.

"The what?" Gary said.

Dusty and I told him what Melody had told us.

"You guys are so full of it," Gary said. "There's no kissing book."

"Ask Melody," I said.

"Is it true?" Gary asked her.

"I really don't know," Melody answered. "But I've heard a lot of girls talk about it."

"Wow." Gary blinked. "If that book's real, I *have* to see what it says."

The next thing we knew, Gary took off back to the eighth-grade jock table where he usually hung out. He started talking and gesturing and in no time the jocks were crowded around him listening.

"Do you believe it?" Dusty asked with a smile.

"The question is, does Gary believe it?" I said. "And the answer looks like yes, he definitely does."

By now Gary was almost completely surrounded by the jocks. We could barely see him in the middle of the crowd. Suddenly, he got up and went over to one of the tables where the eighth-grade girls sat. He started talking to them and the girls started grinning and whispering to each other.

"Check this," Dusty said. "Now he's talking to the girls to see if it's true."

"The dude is seriously gullible," I said.

"What's that mean?" asked Wilson.

"He believes stuff that isn't true," I explained.

"Who said it wasn't true?" Wilson asked. "Maybe the kissing book really does exist."

I crossed my fingers and prayed it didn't.

The next morning my friends and I were back in school early.

"Ready to challenge the long distance chair sliding record?" Dusty asked.

"Ready to get nailed by Monkey Breath?" I asked.

"Not to worry." Wilson opened his backpack and pulled out four small brown corrugated cardboard boxes and a green-and-yellow can of spray starch.

"Antifriction devices," he explained. "Designed to help your chair slide farther and faster than ever before."

He sprayed the bottom of each little box, then put one box on the bottom of each chair leg.

"Why spray starch?" asked Dusty.

Wilson held up the can. "It says right here, 'For a smoother and faster glide.' "

Wilson gave the chair a little push. It slid easily over the tile floor. "Like a hot knife through butter, dudes."

"We'll see." Dusty set the timer on his wristwatch. "Ready?"

Wilson got behind the chair. "Ready."

"Set . . . Go!"

Wilson took off. In no time he'd hopped into the chair and was streaking down the hallway toward the office. Dusty and I ducked around the corner.

By the time the office door opened, Wilson was nowhere in sight. Just as he had the morning before, Principal Monkey Breath charged out into the hall. But this time he didn't stand around scratching his head. He hurried down to the corner and looked around it.

Dusty and I held our breath as we watched.

"He's got to see Wilson," Dusty whispered hoarsely.

"Maybe not," I whispered back.

"No way he could have finished the second hall that fast," Dusty insisted.

"Look out!" someone called behind us.

Dusty and I spun around. It was Wilson in the chair! Dusty and I dove out of the way. Wilson shot past us.

"He's *way* broken the record!" I gasped.

"That's not all he's gonna break," Dusty added.

Wilson showed no sign of stopping. Directly ahead of him was a big glass display case filled with sports trophies.

CRASH!

12

There's nothing like the sound of glass shattering to bring a principal running.

Luckily, Dusty and I got to Wilson first. He was still in the chair. Only both the chair and Wilson were lying on their backs. The floor was covered with small greenish glass crumbs.

"You okay?" Dusty asked.

"Do I *look* okay?" Wilson groaned.

"You're gonna look a lot worse as soon as Monkey Breath gets here," I said. The slapping sound of leather soles was coming closer. I grabbed Wilson's arm and gave him a yank up. Wilson got to his feet, but started to slip on the broken glass crumbs.

"Whoa!" He waved his arms wildly as his feet slid around under him. Meanwhile, the slapping sounds of Monkey Breath's shoes was growing louder.

"Come on, Wilson!" Still holding his arm, I tried to drag him away from the shattered display case. Dusty was pulling the chair away.

"Wait!" Wilson bent down.

"What are you doing?" I asked. "Monkey Breath is gonna come around that corner any second!"

"These are perfect!" Wilson started scooping up handfuls of the shattered glass crumbs.

"Perfect for what?" I asked.

"Antifriction devices."

"In about two seconds you're gonna need an anti-*expulsion* device," I warned him.

The slapping footsteps were loud now. I grabbed Wilson's arm and pulled hard.

"In here!" Dusty held open a door.

I dragged Wilson inside.

The door closed.

"What the devil?!" Monkey Breath shouted out in the hall.

There was no doubt in our minds why he was shouting. He'd just found the smashed display case.

"Who did this?" he shouted. "I know you can't have gone far. Come out right now!"

13

My friends and I stood inside the door, catching our breath.

Creak . . . Slam!

From out in the hall came the sound of doors opening and closing.

"He's searching rooms!" Wilson whispered. "What do we do?"

"Shh!" Dusty and I both pressed our fingers to our lips and hushed him. Then we looked around. We were in the weight-and-exercise room next to the girls locker room. The W&E room was used by upper-grade students and teachers. It had weights, exercise bikes, and treadmills. Along one wall was a rock climbing course that reached all the way to the ceiling.

Creak . . . Slam! The sound of opening and closing doors was coming closer. We could hear Monkey Breath mumbling something about little green women.

"What's with him and little green women?" Dusty whispered.

"Don't know," I whispered back. "But I do know it's time to climb."

If Monkey Breath had bothered to look up when he entered the W&E room, he would have found my friends and me clinging to the wall near the ceiling like tree frogs.

Monkey Breath looked left. He looked right. But he never looked up.

"That was way too close," Wilson groaned later after we'd climbed back down.

Briiiingg! The morning bell rang. School had officially begun for the day.

"Close, but no cigar." Dusty pushed open the door and headed out into the hall. Kids were coming into school carrying backpacks. Gary Gordon was one of them. Dusty winked at me.

"Hey, Gary, what did you find out about the kissing book?" he teased.

Gary narrowed his eyes and frowned. But the frown slowly turned into a smile. "Plenty."

That wasn't the answer we expected. For a

moment, no one said a word. Then Wilson said, "What do you mean?"

"I mean, I read it yesterday after school," Gary said.

"Bull," I said. "You couldn't have read it because it doesn't exist."

"Don't you wish, Kyle," said Gary.

"Why would Kyle wish?" Wilson asked.

"Because if he knew what it said about him he'd wish that book never existed," Gary said.

Wilson stared at me. "Is that true?"

"How would I know if it's true?" I asked.

"It's logic," he said. "You can't be in the book if you haven't kissed a girl. You swore you haven't kissed a girl. Therefore, you can't be in the book, right?"

Instead of answering, I turned to Gary. "You really expect us to believe you snuck into the girls locker room and figured out which locker the book was in and then figured out the combination?"

"No, dummy," Gary replied. "I asked a friend of mine to do it."

"So how'd *he* know which locker and combination?" Wilson asked.

"Because my friend isn't a *he*, you bonehead," Gary snarled. "She's a she."

"I think you're full of it," I insisted. "There's no such book."

35

"It's a small, thick, dark blue spiral notebook," Gary said. "The pages are all dog-eared and bent. Like it's been read a thousand times."

"You're making this up," I said.

"Don't believe me." Gary shrugged and started to walk away.

"Don't listen to him, Kyle," Dusty said. "He's just playing with your head. The whole thing sounds totally bogus."

But twenty feet away, Gary stopped. With a sly smile on his face, he said, "By the way, Kyle, you remember Tara Jones, don't you?"

Suddenly, I felt woozy.

15

It felt as if the blood had just drained out of my head.

"Wasn't Tara Jones that cute girl who moved away last summer?" Wilson asked.

"Gee, Kyle, you look awful pale." Dusty put his hand on my shoulder. "You okay, dude?"

"Huh? Oh, uh, sure," I said. "I don't know what Gary's talking about."

"Now that I think of it," Wilson said, "you and Tara *were* kind of friendly."

"Anyone can be friendly with a girl," I said. "It doesn't mean anything."

"I don't know," Wilson said suspiciously. "I kind of remember you being a little *more* than just friendly with Tara."

"Drop dead," I muttered. "I don't care what Gary says. There's no such book."

"How can you be so sure?" Dusty asked.

"I just am, okay?" I said. "I mean, of all the

dumb things in the world. Why would the girls keep a kissing book in their locker room?"

"Maybe so they could warn other girls about bad kissers," Wilson guessed. "And the girls locker room would be the perfect place because it's the last place the boys could get into to see what it says."

I glanced at Dusty, hoping he'd disagree. But Dusty just shrugged. "I'd say that was a pretty good answer."

"Well, I say it's completely dumb," I shot back. "You could probably ask any girl in this school and they'd tell you the same thing."

Wilson looked past me. "Good idea. And here comes the perfect person."

I spun around. Coming down the hall toward us was Melody.

I felt the hair on the back of my neck stand. Goose bumps raced up and down my arms.

"Okay, listen, guys," I said quickly. "We are not going to talk about this with her, get it? And I *definitely* don't want to hear either of you mention Tara's name."

"Why not?" Wilson asked.

"Because I just don't, okay?" I said.

"But you said you've never kissed a girl," said Wilson. "And since Tara is a girl, that means you never kissed Tara."

"It's logic," Dusty added with a wink.

Before I could respond, Melody joined us. "Hi, handsome." She gave me a warm smile, then turned to Dusty and Wilson. "Hi, guys, how's the search for the mysterious kissing book going?"

"Funny you should mention that," Dusty said.

"It's stupid," I blurted. "There's no such book. It's just a dumb rumor. I mean it, Melody, whatever you hear, don't believe a word."

But Wilson was eyeing me in a suspicious way. "Gee, Kyle, since none of it is true, I guess you won't care if I tell Melody the rumor we heard about you."

Wilson had backed me into a corner. If I argued too hard against him telling Melody about the rumor, it would look like I was trying to hide something.

"Sure, go ahead." I pretended I didn't care.

"Turns out Gary says he actually *saw* the kissing book," Wilson told Melody. "A friend of his went into the girls locker room and got it for him."

Melody's eyebrows rose. "You mean it really exists?"

"Only if you believe a total liar like Gary," I said.

"Right," agreed Dusty.

"So guess who Gary says got a major write-up in the book?" Wilson nodded in my direction.

Melody stared at me with wide eyes. "Really?"

I felt my face grow hot and knew it must have been turning red. Wilson and Dusty were staring at my hands. I looked down and realized I was clenching and unclenching my fists.

"Uh, dude." Dusty started to tug at Wilson's shirtsleeve. "I think it's time we left Kyle and Melody alone, okay?"

"Why?" Wilson asked, glaring at me. "I don't

see what the big deal is. After all, Kyle *couldn't possibly* have anything to hide, could he?"

Dusty pulled harder. "Come on, let's go."

He finally got Wilson to leave. Meanwhile Melody was still gazing at me with her eyebrows raised in a curious way.

"It's total bull, Melody," I said. "Gary made it all up and all Wilson did was repeat it."

"I can see that," Melody said, smiling.

I have to admit that I was pretty annoyed for the rest of the day. By the time I saw Wilson and Dusty, after school ended, I'd pretty much calmed down. But I was still semi-ticked off.

"Thanks a lot, Wilson," I grumbled as we walked down the hall. "Really, thanks a whole bunch."

"I don't see what you're so bent out of shape about," Wilson replied. "After all, *none* of it's true, right?"

"Just can it, okay?" I snapped.

"Hey, come on, both of you," Dusty said. "Give it a rest. Take it easy. I mean, even if there really is a book, so what? And so what if Kyle's in it? So what if it even says something about him and Tara? She moved away. What difference could it make now?"

"Kyle said he's never kissed a girl," Wilson muttered.

"Look, Wilson, let's not get into this again," Dusty said. "There are certain things you don't want people to think about you, whether they're true or not. End of discussion."

We passed the W&E room. Dusty stopped and motioned to Wilson and me. The door was slightly open and we could see inside where Ms. Fortune and Mr. Gutsy were side by side on the exercise bikes. They were riding hard and glistening with sweat. The funny thing was they were so into looking at each other that they didn't even notice us.

My friends and I started down the hall again.

"Did you see the way they were looking at each other?" Wilson made a face. "I mean, teachers in love. It's gross."

"Who else are they supposed to be in love with?" Dusty asked.

"I don't know," Wilson said. "But you'd think they could do it *after* school or something."

"I have news for you," I said. "It is after school."

"Then they should do it *away* from school," Wilson said. "Like somewhere where we won't see them."

Hard Marks is an old school and the entrances to the boys and girls locker rooms aren't inside the gym like at newer schools. Instead, you enter them from the hall. As my friends and I passed the girls locker room, Dusty suddenly stopped near the door and brought his finger to his lips. "Listen."

Wilson and I stopped. From inside the girls locker room we could hear giggles and parts of a conversation:

"Who should we read about next?"

"Did you see what it says about Ricky Cheech?"

Out in the hall, Wilson whispered, "They're reading the book!"

Dusty frowned. "How could Cheech the Leech be in it?"

"Look at this about Gary Gordon," a girl in the locker room said next.

"Are you surprised?" asked another.

"No!"

The giggling grew louder.

"Look what it says about Kyle."

"I know," said someone else. *"Who would have thought?"*

Wilson scowled at me. Just then the door to the girls locker room swung open and out came Rachel Smath. When she saw my friends and me, her eyes went wide and her mouth fell open.

"Oh, my gosh!" she gasped, then turned back into the locker room. "He's right *here*!"

In no time a bunch of girls crowded into the doorway. Alice was one of them. Meanwhile, Rachel screeched, "Put it away!"

Clang! Inside the girls locker room a locker door slammed shut.

"Did you hear?" asked one of the girls in the doorway.

"Not really," said Dusty.

"Maybe a little bit," admitted Wilson.

"That's really low," said Rachel.

"Oh, sure," Dusty scoffed at her. "It's okay for you to write stuff in some book about how boys kiss, but it's not okay for us to wonder what it says?"

"It's okay to wonder," Rachel replied. "It's not okay to eavesdrop." She turned to me. "Especially when it's about one of *you.*"

"Come on, guys," I said. "Let's just go."

We'd started down the hall when someone called out behind us. "Kyle? Wait!"

It was Alice. "You guys think I could talk to Kyle alone?"

Dusty and Wilson started to grin.

"Go on, you dirtballs," I said. "I'll catch up in a second."

Dusty and Wilson headed toward the doors. Alice waited until they were out of earshot. I figured that she wanted to talk to me again about being her coanchor on the morning TV show. You had to give Alice credit. She never gave up.

But that wasn't what she wanted to talk about.

"Kyle," she said, "I just want you to know that I don't believe a word of what that book says about you. And even if it's true, I still don't care."

I felt myself turning pale. "Er, thanks, Alice. Catch you later." I turned and caught up with Dusty and Wilson outside of school. What could it have said?

"What'd Alice want?" Wilson asked as we started home.

"She still wants me to be her coanchor," I lied.

"Fat chance," Dusty said. He and Wilson started talking about other things. I hardly heard them. I couldn't get what Alice had said out of my head. *Even if what the book said about me was true . . .*

How bad could it be?

"I can't believe I'm doing this," I grumbled the next morning. I was waiting for Wilson to finish spraying silicone on the bottoms of the glass-crumb runners he'd built for the chair the night before.

"Don't you want a chance to break the world long distance chair sliding record?" Wilson asked.

"I also have a chance to break my neck and break the all-time Hard Marks Middle School suspension record if Monkey Breath nails me," I pointed out.

"At least you can't break the display case," said Dusty. "It's still broken from yesterday."

"Ready." Wilson stepped away from the chair.

"Set." Dusty adjusted the timer on his wristwatch.

I put my hands on the chair and pushed it slightly. It glided over the floor like a puck in air hockey. The idea of breaking the world long distance chair sliding record was tempting. Very tempting.

"Go!" Wilson said.

I took off, pushing the chair ahead of me. Like a bobsled racer, I hopped on once I'd reached cruising speed. A split second later I was sailing down the hall. I even leaned forward to cut down on wind resistance. This was seriously cool!

All I had to do was get past the office and around the corner without getting caught.

The office was coming up fast.

There was no sign of Monkey Breath.

And —

Suddenly, something caught me. The chair slowed so fast I practically fell out. I looked down. A thick black band of rubber had caught the front two legs of my chair. The rubber spanned one side of the hall to the other. It was stretching back like a slingshot.

Sproing! The slingshot fired.

The next thing I knew I was going backward . . . back up the hall at incredible speed.

In no time I shot past Dusty and Wilson.

Crash! I hit something behind me.

I felt it.

I heard it.

But strangely, it only slowed me down.

And then I knew why.

Because I *smelled* it!

I'd just smashed open the door to the boys' room!

The ride became bumpy as the chair rattled over the tiny tiles. I passed the urinals and stalls.

Clank! The chair hit the radiator and came to a stop.

For a second I just sat there trying to understand what had happened. Then the boys' room door burst open and Dusty and Wilson ran in.

"It's a trap!" Wilson gasped.

"Monkey Breath's coming!" cried Dusty.

20

Luckily, we were experienced at hiding in the stalls. The trick was to stand on the toilet so anyone who ducked down wouldn't see your feet on the floor. Kids were always going into the stalls and locking them from the inside and then crawling out.

Dusty and Wilson each went into a stall. I went into a third stall, picked up the chair, and put it on the toilet and then sat on the chair. A second later the door swung open. The evil Dr. Monkey Breath had arrived.

My friends and I held our breath.

One of the advantages of having a short principal is that he isn't tall enough to stretch up and look over the stall doors. Nor would he dare get down on his hands and knees on the boys' room's gross floor and look under them.

"It's you, isn't it?" Monkey Breath grumbled. "You little green women. Hiding in the boys' room. Well, fine, stay here."

We heard footsteps. The door creaked open and closed, but none of us moved a muscle. One of Monkey Breath's favorite tricks is pretending to leave the bathroom and then suddenly bursting back in.

Sure enough, a second later the boys' room door swung open. But strangely, the person who entered started to hum to himself, and didn't sound at all like our principal. Curious to see who it was, I silently rose up on the chair and peeked over the top of the stall.

It was Cheech the Leech!

Wilson and Dusty were also peeking over their stall doors. Cheech strolled up to the mirror. He glanced to his left and right as if making double sure no one else was around. Then he ran some water into his hands and used his fingers to push and pull his hair, as if trying to make it perfect. All the while he kept humming to himself.

Finally, when he'd finished with his hair, he pulled out a little canister of breath spray and shot it into his mouth. Still watching from the stalls, Dusty, Wilson, and I glanced at each other and smiled.

"Lookin' good, stud," Cheech said to himself in the mirror. "Can't wait for Friday night."

"I bet you can't, stud," Dusty said.

Cheech spun around and stared up at us. His mouth fell open.

"Just what makes you think a cool haircut and

some mouth spray is gonna make any girl want to kiss you?" Dusty asked.

Just when you expected Cheech to narrow his eyes angrily and spit out something nasty, he smiled. "I'm gonna get you for this, Dusty."

"Yeah, right." Dusty chuckled.

"I mean it." Cheech winked.

"How?" Dusty asked.

"You'll see." Cheech turned and strolled out of the boys' room, whistling happily as if he had everything under control.

A moment later Dusty, Wilson, and I left the boys' room.

"What's with him?" I asked.

"I don't know," Dusty said.

"It's like he knows something we don't know," said Wilson.

"Unless it's a bluff," speculated Dusty.

"I don't think so," I said. "We totally caught him by surprise back there. He'd have to be thinking really fast to come up with that if it wasn't true."

No one said a thing. It made us all nervous to think that Cheech knew stuff we didn't know.

"You're not going to tell everyone what he did in the bathroom, are you?" I asked.

"Naw." Dusty shook his head.

"Why not?" asked Wilson.

" 'Cause everybody does dumb stuff in the mirror when they think they're alone," Dusty said.

"It's like the fine line between goofing around and being really mean," I said.

"Yeah, I guess you guys are right." Wilson shrugged. "I wouldn't want anyone to do anything like that to me."

Dusty nodded. "Besides, I'm not so sure I want to get Cheech really mad at us. I don't know what he knows, but I don't want him using it against us."

Wilson had to go down to the TV studio for Alice's morning show. Dusty and I went into homeroom. When Cheech saw us, he smiled and waved. Dusty and I shared a bewildered look. The kid was definitely acting freaky.

We took our seats and didn't say a word. Ms. Taylor turned on the TV and the morning show began with Alice sitting at the news desk and making a dramatic plea for the return of the master gym locker key.

"So far there have been no reports of anything being stolen from either the girls' or boys' gym lockers," she reported. "However, Principal Chump feels that the person who has the key may be waiting until everyone forgets about it. Therefore, he told me this morning that unless the key is returned by the end of the school day this Friday, he will cancel the overnight camping trip to Squeegee Lake and use the money to replace the locks."

The morning show ended. No sooner did the TV go off than the PA speaker over the door crackled on: "Dusty Lane, Wilson Kriss, and Kyle Brawly to the principal's office immediately."

Dusty and I picked up our backpacks and headed for the door. Out in the hall, we ran into Wilson, who was coming from the TV studio.

"You think Monkey Breath figured out we're behind the long distance chair sliding?" Wilson asked.

"I don't know how," I said.

"That has to be it," Dusty said. "What else have we done wrong?"

We went into the office and sat down on the bench to wait. Wilson started gnawing on this thumbnail, his feet tapping crazily against the floor.

"Relax, dude," Dusty said. "It's not that serious."

"Maybe it's something else," Wilson replied. "Something we don't know about."

"Chair abuse?" I guessed with a smile.

"How about destroying glass display cases?" Wilson asked.

Dusty and I shared a nervous look. We'd forgotten about that. For once, maybe we did have something to worry about.

The main office door opened and Ms. Fortune skipped in with a big smile on her face. "Oh, hello, boys, what did you do now?" she asked cheerfully, as if she were commenting on what a beautiful day it was.

"Uh, er, we're not sure," Dusty answered.

"Well, good luck!" Ms. Fortune skipped away.

"That is really gross," Wilson groaned.

"Love among teachers?" I asked.

Wilson nodded. "There ought to be a law against it."

The door to the evil Dr. Monkey Breath's private dungeon opened, and there stood Monkey Breath with a glower on his face. "Come in, boys."

We went in. The curtains in Monkey Breath's dungeon are always closed, so it's really dim and hard to see. The walls are covered with egg-crate soundproofing. My friends and I started to take our usual seats.

"Stop," Monkey Breath ordered. He took something out of his desk. It kind of looked like a long black flashlight, only without the wide lightbulb part. "Stand with your legs apart and your arms out."

22

My friends and I did as we were told. Monkey Breath went over our bodies with the wand thing.

"Looking for weapons?" Dusty joked.

"Don't be silly," Monkey Breath grumbled.

"Then what are you looking for?" I asked.

"Hidden mikes," our principal answered.

"You're worried we're gonna tape you?" Wilson realized.

"You can't be too careful these days." Monkey Breath finished with the wand and went behind his desk again. He took out three sheets of paper. "I'd like each of you to sign one of these."

"What are they?" I asked. The sheets looked like some kind of form.

"Confidentiality agreements," Monkey Breath replied. "By signing them you're agreeing that nothing said inside this office will be repeated to anyone. Is that clear?"

Wilson and I nodded and started to sign our names.

"Wait a minute," Dusty said. "Does that mean that if we don't sign them you won't talk to us?"

"That's correct," Monkey Breath replied.

Dusty grinned. "Don't sign them, guys."

Wilson and I straightened up. Dusty was right. If we didn't sign, Monkey Breath couldn't talk to us. Our principal must have realized this, too, because he scowled and rubbed his chin thoughtfully. Then he let out a big sigh, thus releasing a horrible cloud of toxic Monkey Breath. I wanted to barf. Wilson started to sway as if he might faint.

"Okay, boys, forget the agreements," Monkey Breath finally said. "Just sit down."

We sat. Monkey Breath stood in front of his desk with his arms crossed. No one said anything, although I was tempted to ask why his hair was all crazy and his eye was twitching and who the little green women were.

"Do you know why you're here, boys?" our principal finally asked.

My friends and I glanced at each other. We were pretty sure it had something to do with breaking the display case. Only if we said that, we were basically admitting guilt.

"Not a clue," Dusty said.

"Take a guess," Monkey Breath said.

"Uh, because . . . you miss us?" Wilson guessed.

Monkey Breath shook his head.

"You're lonely?" Dusty guessed.

Again our principal shook his head. "I'll give you a hint. It has something to do with a missing key."

"**B**ut — " I started to say.
"No buts!" Monkey Breath growled. "Yes or no, but no buts."

Usually when Monkey Breath accused us of something, there was at least a tiny bit of truth to it. But this time, he couldn't have been more wrong.

I raised my hand.

"Yes, Kyle?" said Monkey Breath.

"May I speak frankly, and above all, honestly on this matter without using the word *but*?" I asked.

Monkey Breath's eye twitched. "Go ahead."

"Sir, I totally and completely swear that my friends and I have nothing to do with that missing key," I said. "We don't know where it is, and we don't know who could possibly have it. Frankly, while we may cause a lot of trouble around here, stealing stuff is not our style."

Monkey Breath blinked both eyes several times.

"In addition," I went on, "I might point out that as far as my associates and I know, there is nothing one could find in a gym locker that would be worth the cancellation of our annual overnight camping trip to Squeegee Lake."

"Not scuzzy socks," added Wilson.

"Nor overripe T-shirts," said Dusty.

"So it really doesn't seem — "

"Ha!" Without warning, Monkey Breath spun around and jumped out of his chair as if he thought someone was sneaking up behind him. "I've got you!"

Of course, no one was. He frowned and appeared puzzled. Then he sat down again and faced us.

"Who have you got?" Wilson asked him.

"Forget about it," Monkey Breath answered. "You were saying, Kyle?"

I told him my friends and I didn't think it was fair to cancel the trip.

"We searched the cafeteria and Ms. Mopp found all the other keys," Monkey Breath pointed out.

"It still could be lost," I said. "It could have slipped into a crack or gotten stuck to the bottom of someone's shoe without them noticing."

"If any other key was missing, I might agree with you," Monkey Breath replied. "However, when the master key is the only one missing, I have to suspect foul play. However, I will not make my final decision until Friday afternoon. So the best way to guarantee that you get to go on that trip is to find that key, boys."

Now Dusty raised his hand. "Excuse me, sir, but . . . er, I mean, are you actually *suggesting* that my friends and I, who are often and incorrectly considered three of the biggest troublemakers in school, *help* you find the key?"

"I think that would be a superb idea," Monkey Breath replied.

"You're *deputizing* us?" Wilson said in amazement.

"That's one way to look at it."

"Why us?" I asked.

Monkey Breath leaned forward so that we could experience the full impact of his horrible breath. His eye twitched and he blinked several times. "Because we're looking for a troublemaker, boys. And it takes one to know one."

"**N**ow there's a shocking concept," I said as we left the office.

"Yeah," said Wilson. "Imagine Monkey Breath asking *us* for help."

"Kind of like the fire department asking an arsonist to help prevent fires," Dusty quipped.

"Or a bakery asking Cookie Monster to guard their cookies," said Wilson.

"Smells like reverse psychology to me," I said. "Like your mom telling you that you can't do something she wants you to do because she knows that'll make you really want to do it."

"That's not what reverse psychology is," said Dusty.

"Oh, yeah?" I raised an eyebrow. "What do *you* think it is?"

"Ygolohcysp."

"You're just a laugh and a half, Dusty," I smirked. "But — "

"No buts," Wilson reminded me.

"Just butt ox and butt brains," added Dusty.

"Seriously, dudes," I said. "We have a problem. If kids find out we're helping Monkey Breath, our reputation is sunk."

"Except for one thing," said Dusty.

"What's that?" asked Wilson.

"Are we really helping him?"

My friends and I stopped and looked at each other. The answer was obvious.

No way.

25

At lunch Gary was standing in the middle of the cafeteria talking to Melody.

"What do you think that's about?" Dusty whispered as we came out of the lunch line.

"Who cares?" I shrugged.

"Come on." The next thing I knew, Dusty was tiptoeing up behind them.

"Seriously, Melody," Gary was saying. "It's gonna be a cool party. You really should go."

"You hoping Melody will give you a good write-up in the kissing book?" Dusty teased him.

Gary spun around with a surprised look on his face.

Melody laughed. "All you guys are too much!" She started away. "Catch you later."

After she left, Gary glared at us. "I couldn't get anything worse than the write-up *you* got, Dusty."

For a moment Dusty was speechless. "No way," he finally croaked.

"Does the name Brittany ring a bell?" Gary asked.

"I don't know what you're talking about," Dusty said.

"Too bad," chuckled Gary. "Because it really sounded like Brittany knew what *she* was talking about."

He walked away. Wilson and I kept our eyes on Dusty.

"What're you guys looking at?" he growled and started toward our regular table. Wilson and I followed and put down our trays. Dusty usually dives right into his lunch. Today he just sat staring at it. He definitely wasn't acting like King Calm, the easygoing guy we usually hung around with.

"Something wrong?" Wilson asked.

"Gary's crazy," Dusty grumbled. "I don't know anyone named Brittany."

"Yes, you do," I said. "Rachel Smath's cousin, remember? She stayed with Rachel for a couple of weeks at the end of last summer."

"Her name was Brit," Dusty said.

"Short for Brittany," I said.

Dusty's mouth fell open. You could see he'd just put Brit and Brittany together. It was kind of funny. Dusty was usually as easygoing as anyone you ever met. Now he looked like a rat trapped in a cage.

"So it's true?" Wilson asked.

"No comment," Dusty muttered.

Wham! Wilson banged his fist against the lunch table angrily. "I can't believe it!"

Dusty and I were startled.

"What's with you?" I asked.

"You and Dusty are *both* in that stupid book!" Wilson complained. "You lied to me. You swore you'd never kiss girls."

Dusty and I glanced at each other sheepishly. Neither of us knew what to say. Finally, in a voice hardly more than a whisper, Dusty said, "It's not the kind of stuff you go around broadcasting, dude."

"And it's not true anyway," I added.

"Yeah, right," Wilson said bitterly. "That's why every time someone mentions the kissing book both of you start looking like a couple of deer caught in the headlights." He shook his head. "I just can't *get over* you guys. All that moaning and groaning about how you wouldn't kiss a girl if your lives depended on it. And I *believed* you! I mean, am I a total butt ox, or what?"

I couldn't help smiling a little. "What would you have done differently?"

"Go stick your head in a toilet," Wilson grumbled. "I thought you guys were my best friends."

Meanwhile, Dusty had started drumming his fingers against the table. "I hate to say it, but now I have to find out what's in that book."

"How?" I asked.

Dusty nodded at something behind me. I turned and saw Melody sitting with her friends, talking and laughing.

"That's how," he said.

"**W**ait a minute," I said. "I don't want Melody involved in this."

"Why not?" asked Wilson.

"I just don't, okay?"

"You worried about what she might read in the book?" Dusty asked with a smile.

"I thought you said nothing in the book was true," said Wilson.

"Darn right," I said.

"So just tell her that," Dusty said.

"Why can't we just leave it alone?" I asked.

"I don't know about you, partner," Dusty said in a low voice, "but I would find it hard to walk through the halls thinking that girls are reading stuff about me. *Especially* stuff that might not be true."

I felt cornered. No matter what I said, it meant trouble. Meanwhile, Dusty waved. "Hey, Melody?"

She looked over at us. "Yes?"

"Think we could talk to you for a second?"

Melody came over. "Sure, guys, what's up?"

"We need a huge favor," Dusty said.

"Dusty needs a huge favor," I corrected him.

"What kind of favor?" asked Melody.

"It's kind of private," said Dusty.

Melody sat down and huddled with us over the lunch table.

"We need you to find out the locker and get the combination of the lock," Wilson said. It was kind of funny to hear him say this, since we knew he wasn't in the book. You had to figure he wanted to feel like he was involved.

"What locker?" Melody asked.

"The one with the book," Dusty said.

"The kissing book?" Melody asked.

Dusty nodded.

"I thought you said it doesn't exist," Melody said.

"There's been new evidence in the case," said Dusty.

Melody frowned.

"There's something in the book Dusty needs to know about," Wilson explained.

Melody smiled. "You think you've been written up?"

Dusty actually started to blush. I'm not sure I'd ever seen him do that before.

"And you want to know what it says?" Melody asked.

Dusty nodded.

"Why do you want me to get you the locker number and combination?" Melody asked. "Wouldn't it be a lot easier if I just read the book and told you what it says?"

"No!" I blurted.

Dusty smiled at me. "Why not, Kyle?"

"I, uh, just don't think it's right to ask Melody to do that," I said.

"Oh, I wouldn't mind," Melody said. "Actually I'm kind of curious myself."

"You really, *really* don't want to," I said.

"I don't?" Melody asked, surprised.

"You're not that kind of girl," I tried to explain. "You don't want people thinking you're actually interested in stuff like that, do you?"

"I really don't care what people think," Melody replied.

I could see I was only getting into more trouble. I took a deep breath. "Look, Melody, all we want is the locker number and combination, okay? If you can get us that, you'll be doing us a really big favor."

"Well, okay, if that's all you want." Melody got up and left. As soon as she was gone, Dusty got in my face.

"What good is the combination going to do us?" he asked.

"What do you mean?" I asked.

"I mean, how are we going to know what's in

that book if we don't ask Melody to read it for us?" he said.

"We'll read it ourselves," I said.

"It's in the girls locker room, dummy," said Wilson.

"I know," I said.

"The only way we can read it ourselves is if we go in there ourselves," Wilson pointed out.

"Right," I said.

Dusty and Wilson both stared at me. "You want to go *into* the girls locker room?"

"No," I said. "I don't *want* to. But I will if I *have* to."

27

One does not undertake a mission like entering the girls locker room without serious planning and preparation. By sixth period that afternoon Melody had provided us with the vital information. The locker's number was 397. Its combination was 6-27-14.

My friends and I stayed until after-school activities and sports ended. Today would be a practice run. As we neared the girls locker room we could hear voices.

"Someone's in the locker room," Wilson whispered.

"Not the locker room," Dusty whispered back. "The W&E room."

My friends and I snuck up to the door. Inside, Ms. Fortune and Mr. Gutsy were sitting side by side on the exercise bikes, pedaling and talking as they worked up sweats.

"What do we do about them?" I whispered to Dusty.

"Hopefully they won't be here tomorrow," he whispered back.

Wilson brought a stopwatch. The idea was to see how much time passed between when the last girl left the locker room and when Sam the custodian came in to clean up.

"Twenty minutes," Wilson said.

"That's enough time," Dusty said.

"Barely," I said.

"Why barely?" Dusty asked.

"We're talking about sneaking in," I said. "Finding the right locker, unlocking it, going through the book . . . I mean, it's not like you and I are the only guys they've ever written about, Dusty. There could be pages and pages. Then reading whatever it is they have written, then putting the book back, locking the locker, and getting out without being seen."

"Sounds like a mission!" Wilson gasped. "Mission Impossible!"

"More like Mission Im*probable*," I said.

"Whatever." Wilson shrugged.

"Look, I've got news for you," Dusty said. "We're running out of time. Tomorrow's Thursday. The next day is Friday. You know what Friday is?"

"The day before Saturday?" Wilson guessed.

"The day of the big party, idiot," Dusty said.

"It's also the day Monkey Breath cancels the

overnight if he hasn't gotten the master key back," I said.

I stared at the girls locker room. Inside was a strange land, a dangerous and alien world to any boy. I sighed. "All right, men. Tomorrow we go in."

28

We agreed that long distance chair sliding would have to be postponed the next morning while we focused on Mission Improbable. Instead of walking to school early, we met at the bus stop.

"Where's Wilson?" I asked.

"Don't know," answered Dusty. He popped some M&M's into his mouth that he'd just collected from the Five Dwarfs, who were the single-digit little kids we rode the bus with.

Suddenly, the dwarf pod started twittering. Dusty and I turned around and saw why. Wilson was coming down the sidewalk toward us wearing green-and-brown camouflage clothes. He'd even rubbed blacking on his face.

"I don't believe it," Dusty groaned.

"What are you doing?" I asked Wilson.

"Going on a mission," he answered excitedly.

"Do you have to announce it to the whole school?" I asked.

Wilson blinked. "Gee."

"Hadn't thought of that, huh?" Dusty said.

Wilson shook his head. "It's too late to go home and change."

"At least wash the junk off your face when we get to school," I said.

The bus came and we went to school. In homeroom we talked to our friends while on Hart TV Alice begged everyone not to forget about the recycling competition and to keep an eye out for the master key to the locker room lockers.

The day passed slowly. All I could think about was Mission Improbable. Once again we waited until the after-school activities and sports were over. Today wasn't a practice run. This was the real thing.

"Come on," Dusty whispered as he led us down the empty hall outside the girls locker room. Suddenly, he froze and pressed his finger against his lips. Wilson and I stopped and listened. We could hear voices inside the W&E room.

It was Ms. Fortune and Mr. Gutsy. Once again they were pedaling side by side on the exercise bicycles, their faces glistening with sweaty love among teachers.

"Darn," Wilson whispered. "What do we do now?"

"Don't sweat it," Dusty answered. "They're in

totally oblivious love land. They won't notice a thing."

"You sure?" I whispered.

"No, I'm not sure," Dusty whispered back. "But we're committed to this mission and I say we follow through."

"Okay," I whispered, "let's go."

"Wait!" Wilson gasped.

Dusty and I stopped. "Now what?"

"Don't you want to synchronize watches?" he asked.

Dusty rolled his eyes. "If you don't stop it, I'm going to synchronize your nose. Now come on!"

We reached the door to the girls locker room. Dusty paused and stared at it. Inside was enemy territory, a place where few if any young men had ever ventured.

Dusty took a deep breath and pushed on the door. We tiptoed in. The room smelled faintly of perfume, and the gym lockers weren't as scratched or dented as the ones in the boys locker room.

Wilson stopped and shivered.

"What's wrong?" I whispered.

"I don't know," he whispered back. "This place just gives me the creeps."

"It's *supposed* to give you the creeps," Dusty hissed. "Now come on, let's find that locker."

It wasn't as easy as you might think. The girls

locker room was filled with rows of lockers, but they weren't in any order. My friends and I split up and went up and down the rows.

"Found it!" Dusty whispered.

Wilson and I hurried to join him. Dusty dug a piece of paper out of his pocket. The numbers 6-27-14 were written on it.

"How much time do we have?" he whispered as he started to do the combination on the lock.

Neither Wilson nor I answered.

Dusty looked at Wilson. "I asked you how much time is left."

"How would I know?" Wilson asked back.

"You're supposed to be keeping the time," Dusty sputtered.

"We never synchronized our watches," Wilson said.

"You don't have to synchronize watches to know when twenty minutes is up!" Dusty hissed. "All you have to do is know what time it was when we came in here."

"Well, *you* didn't want to synchronize watches so I didn't bother checking," Wilson huffed.

"That's great, Wilson," Dusty grumbled. "Just great. Thanks for the help."

"Chill, guys," I whispered. "Let's get this over with and get out of here."

Dusty turned back to the lock. "Darn, now I forgot where I was."

"Start over," I said.

Dusty spun the dial on the lock and did the combination again.

Clink! He yanked the lock open and opened the locker. It was empty. Almost. Lying on the bottom was a thick blue spiral notebook with worn, frayed edges.

29

For a moment, my friends and I just stared at it without saying a word. As if we were having a hard time believing that it actually existed.

"Unreal," Dusty muttered, then reached into the locker and took out the notebook. But he didn't open it right away.

"Come on, open it!" Wilson urged him.

"Chill, dude. You're not even in it."

"How do *you* know?" Wilson jutted his chin out forcefully.

Dusty and I gave him a curious look. "Something you haven't told us?"

"Maybe."

Dusty and I waited for Wilson to say something more, but he didn't.

"Okay, just read it already," he sputtered.

Dusty opened the notebook and started to turn the pages slowly. I had the feeling that now that he had the book he wasn't so eager to read the part about him.

"Look what it says about Kurt Dunn," he said, pausing halfway through the notebook.

"We don't care what it says about Kurt Dunn," Wilson said. "We care what it says about you. Now quit stalling."

"Okay, okay, you don't have to be such a noodge." Dusty started to slowly turn the pages again.

"Will you give me that?" Wilson grabbed the notebook out of his hands. "At this rate we'll be here all night."

Wilson turned to the back of the notebook and started to thumb through the pages quickly. "Let's see. Okay! Here we go! 'Report on Dusty Lane.' "

Just then a voice behind us said, "What in the world are you boys doing in here?"

30

It was Ms. Fortune. Wearing tight black spandex exercise clothes, she was standing at the end of the row of lockers. She had a white towel around her neck and her face was red from exercise.

Without a word, Wilson slowly started to put the book back in the locker.

"Wait a minute." Our assistant principal held out her hand. "Let me see that."

"See what?" Wilson asked.

"Wilson Kriss, you give me that notebook right now," Ms. Fortune commanded.

Wilson handed her the notebook. Ms. Fortune slid it under her arm. "I can't tell you how disappointed I am in you three. I know you like to have good-natured fun, but I would never have guessed that you'd be the ones who took the master key. I want you boys to leave school immediately. I'm sure Principal Chump will have plenty to say to you tomorrow morning."

Ms. Fortune thought we'd taken the master key! Things looked bad. Actually, they looked worse than bad. They looked terrible. Ms. Fortune was the one friend we had in the school administration. If we lost her, we were sunk. I knew I had to do some fast talking.

"We don't have the key," I said.

Ms. Fortune glanced at the locker and then back at me. "Then how did you open this locker?"

I told her the combination and how we knew which locker it was.

"But why would you want to get into this locker?" she asked.

Dusty pointed at the notebook she was holding. "That's the reason."

Ms. Fortune looked down at the book. Then, to our total horror, she opened it and began to read!

We watched in terror as our assistant principal

scowled. Then smiled. Then shook her head. Then chuckled.

"Well, Dusty and Kyle," she said with a grin, "I can see why you were so eager to get your hands on this book. I assume you planned to burn it, or at least tear out the pages that refer to you."

I winced. "Are they *that* bad?"

"All I'll say is that some of your fellow students received far better reviews than you two."

"Ouch!" Dusty yelped. "*That* hurts."

Ms. Fortune nodded. "I'm a bit surprised myself. Not only by the poor reviews some of the more popular boys received, but by some of the glowing remarks made about young men you wouldn't expect to find in a book like this. Ricky Cheech, for example."

My friends and I shared a puzzled glance.

"Are you sure about that?" I asked.

"It says right here," our assistant principal replied. "In fact he's mentioned more than once. He got several excellent reviews."

"From who?" asked Dusty.

"Oh, I really can't tell you that," said Ms. Fortune.

"Do the names at least sound familiar?" I asked.

Ms. Fortune thumbed through the book again. "Well, no. They're not girls who go to this school. He must have met them somewhere else."

She closed the book. "Anyway, boys, I think I'll put this book somewhere safe. And as far as you being in the girls locker room, I'm going to assume it will never, ever happen again. Okay?"

"Definitely," I said.

"I want you all to promise that from now on you'll be supergood," Ms. Fortune said.

"Positively," said Dusty.

Ms. Fortune waved the kissing book before our eyes. "If you can't keep that promise, I may have to tell Principal Chump about this."

"We promise."

"Fine, you can go," Ms. Fortune said.

My friends and I started to leave.

"And if you hear anything about that missing key," Ms. Fortune called behind us, "I expect you to tell me."

My friends and I left school and started to walk home.

"Good thing we were nailed by Ms. Fortune and not the evil Dr. Monkey Breath," Dusty said.

"That's for sure," said Wilson.

"What about all those great reviews Cheech got?" I asked.

"Right." Dusty chuckled. "From girls no one's ever heard of."

"Of all the unlikely butt oxen," Wilson said. "Cheech the Leech. It's like a joke. It's — "

A thought hit Dusty and me at the same time. We both stopped walking. Wilson stopped and turned around. "What's with you guys?"

"You thinking what I'm thinking?" Dusty asked me.

"I think so," I said. "That morning in the boys' room Cheech was fixing his hair and I goofed on him."

"And then the next day Gary told us there was

bad stuff in the kissing book about you," said Dusty.

"Then *you* gave him a hard time about his hair and the mouthwash," I said, "and he said he'd get you back."

"And the next day there was bad stuff in the book about *me*," said Dusty.

"You guys think *Cheech* wrote those things about you in the kissing book?" Wilson asked.

I nodded. "Remember how he kept smiling and acting like he knew something we didn't know?"

"He knew he could get us back big-time," Dusty said.

"What really clinches it for me isn't so much the bad stuff in that book about us — " I began.

"As much as the good stuff about Cheech," Dusty finished the sentence for me.

"You think he wrote *that*, too?" Wilson gasped.

"Think about it, Wilson," Dusty said. "What girl would kiss Cheech the Leech and admit it?"

"Much less write about it," I added.

"Gee." Wilson bit his lip. "When you put it *that* way, you're right. But how'd he get into the girls' . . ." Wilson didn't bother to finish his own sentence. The answer was obvious. "He's the one who's got the key!"

33

The problem: We had less than twenty-four hours to get the master locker room key from Cheech or the overnight camping trip would be canceled.

The solution: ?

That night my phone rang. It was Dusty.

"How're we gonna do it?" he asked.

"Not a clue," I answered. "I've been sitting here trying to come up with something and I just can't."

"Want to do a three-way with Wilson?"

"Sure." I punched in the code for a three-way call and then dialed Wilson's phone number. The phone rang and rang. Finally Wilson picked up. He was breathing hard. "Hello?"

"Dude," I said. "I was just about to hang up."

"Sorry," Wilson apologized. "I was in the basement working on new runners for the long distance chair sliding world record."

"Forget chair sliding," Dusty said. "We have to get Cheech to give up the key."

"Is that all?" Wilson said.

"Very funny," I grumbled. "We're serious."

"So am I," said Wilson. "Meet me in school tomorrow morning, early. We've got some long distance chair sliding to do."

"Didn't you hear what Dusty said?" I asked. "This isn't about chair sliding anymore. It's about getting the master key from Cheech."

"Darn right," Wilson said. "That's why I'll see you guys in the morning. Now if you'll excuse me, I have some runners to work on."

He hung up.

34

Early the next morning Wilson was waiting for us in the hall.

"Okay, guys, let's go." He went into a classroom to get the chair.

"Wilson, I told you this ain't about chair sliding anymore," I said. "It's about getting the key from Cheech."

"Right." Wilson bent down and started putting the runners on the chair legs.

"Listen up, Wilson," Dusty said. "I don't know what you think you're doing, but it's Friday and if we don't get that key by the end of the day, the overnight to Squeegee Lake is going to be canceled."

"Affirmative," Wilson said as he sprayed silicone on the glass crumb runners. "Ready, Dusty?"

"For what?" Dusty asked.

"To create a distraction."

Y ou didn't have to be a rocket scientist to understand Wilson's plan.

But it definitely would have helped.

Wilson wanted Dusty to ride the chair to the big black rubber band trap in front of the office. On the way, he was supposed to shift his weight so that the chair slowly turned until he was going backward.

That meant that when the chair hit the rubber band, he would be facing the other way. Then, when Monkey Breath came out of the office and gave chase, Dusty would be able to get around the corner and lead Monkey Breath around to the other side of the school while Wilson and I installed the old Lunch Lady Cam in the girls locker room, aimed at locker number 397.

"What do I do after I lead Monkey Breath over to the other side of the school?" Dusty asked.

"I don't know," Wilson said.

"Why can't he lead him all the way around and back to this side?" I asked.

"No way," Wilson said. "We'll be in the girls locker room installing the camera. If Monkey Breath's on this side of the school he might catch us."

"But if I keep him on the other side of the school he may catch me," Dusty pointed out.

"Look, how important is this mission to you?" Wilson asked.

"Not very important," Dusty replied.

"Wrong answer," said Wilson. "Every mission is important. It's a small step for mankind, but a giant leap for something else."

"What?" I asked.

"Don't ask so many questions," Wilson grumbled.

36

Being brave and fearless, Dusty took off down the hall with the chair. After he jumped on it, he slowly twisted around until he was facing us.

A second later he hit the big black rubber band. His head was thrown back as the band stretched and stretched . . .

Sproing! The band launched him back in our direction.

Wilson and I ducked around a corner.

The office door flew open and Monkey Breath jumped out and gave chase. We could hear his leather shoes slapping against the floor.

When Dusty got to the corner, he jumped off the chair, started pushing it to pick up speed, and jumped on again. By the time Monkey Breath reached the corner, Dusty was at the far end of the hall, turning again.

Wilson and I broke for the girls locker room. The old Lunch Lady Cam was a small black-and-white television camera Wilson had rigged to catch the Lunch Monitors from H.E.L.L. eating dessert first. Now I helped him mount it high on the wall near locker 397.

We finished the installation a split second before the morning bell rang. We got out into the hall just before the first kids entered school. Wilson headed for the TV station and I went to homeroom.

Everything *appeared* to be proceeding according to plan.

It wasn't until homeroom that I realized something was wrong.

Dusty wasn't there.

37

I found Wilson in the hall after homeroom.

"Ready for part two?" he asked eagerly.

"Negative. We have a problem." I told him that Dusty had not shown up for homeroom. "There's only one other place he can be — the office."

"Darn," Wilson muttered. "Getting caught wasn't part of the plan."

"No, duh," I said.

Wilson tugged at his earlobe. "We have to spring him."

"From the office?" I asked in disbelief.

"Where else?"

"Are you insane?" I asked.

"Did George Washington desert his men at Valley Forge?" Wilson asked as we headed down the hall.

"No, but — "

"Did Winston Churchill let the British surrender in World War Two?"

"I guess not."

"Did Booger give up the fight in *Revenge of the Nerds, Part Four*?" Wilson asked.

"I don't know," I answered. "I never saw it."

"Then rent it," Wilson said as he pushed open the office door.

As Wilson and I went into the office, Ms. Fortune was coming out. "What are you boys doing?" she asked.

"We want to see Principal Chump," Wilson answered.

Ms. Fortune frowned. "I'm sorry, I must have misunderstood you. I could have sworn you said you *wanted* to see Principal Chump."

Wilson and I nodded.

"You mean, he doesn't want to see you? You want to see him?"

"You got it," said Wilson.

Ms. Fortune shook her head and sighed. "Now I've *really* seen everything."

Our assistant principal left. We told one of the office secretaries why we were there.

"I'm sorry," she said. "Principal Chump is busy."

"Not too busy for us," Wilson said.

"I think he is," said the secretary.

"Please tell him that we can give him the master key to all his problems," I said.

She pushed a button on her intercom. A moment later the evil Dr. Monkey Breath slowly opened the door to the dungeon. His hair was wild and his eyes bugged out. He craned his neck and gazed around as if he was looking for something. Then he opened the door a bit wider. "Come in, boys. Hurry."

We went in. Monkey Breath quickly slammed the door behind us. Dusty was sitting inside.

"Hey, dude, what are you doing in here?" Wilson asked innocently.

"I caught him chair sliding," Monkey Breath said as he went around to his desk. His suit was wrinkled and his shirt had food stains on it. It looked like he hadn't changed clothes all week. "I have a sneaking suspicion you already know that, Wilson."

"What makes you say that?" Wilson asked.

With his eyes twitching uncontrollably, Monkey Breath held up one of the glass crumb runners. "Look familiar?"

Wilson swallowed nervously. I was beginning to wonder if he really had a plan after all.

"I can explain," Wilson said.

Monkey Breath blinked repeatedly. "This I'd like to hear."

"It's all part of our plan to get the key back for you," Wilson said.

Monkey Breath gave him a suspicious look. "You *know* who has the key?"

"Yes," said Wilson.

"No," I blurted.

Wilson frowned at me. "What are you talking about? We know exactly — "

"How to *find out* who has the key," I said quickly.

"But — " Wilson began.

"No buts," snapped Monkey Breath.

"We'd really hate to see *anyone* get into serious trouble," I said. "Even someone we might not be best friends with. Even someone who may have gone out of his way to write things that would make him look good and Dusty and me look bad."

"We would?" Wilson repeated with a frown, then understood. "Oh, yeah, we would."

"I'm afraid you're too late for that," Monkey Breath informed us. "Your friend Dusty here is already in serious trouble for chair sliding."

"Is that against the rules?" I asked innocently.

"Of course it is," Monkey Breath sputtered. "I mean, it must be. It *has* to be."

But even as the words left his mouth, we could see him start to doubt. All the school rules were kept in thick blue ring binders on the shelf behind Monkey Breath's desk. Our principal pulled the one marked *School and Cafeteria Rules* off the shelf and started to read through it.

"Aha!" He plunged his finger down. "It says right here that school furniture is to be used only for its intended purpose. Sliding down the hall at a high rate of speed is not the purpose a chair was intended for."

"You're right," said Wilson. "Chairs are made for sitting and that is precisely what Dusty was doing in his."

"He wasn't sitting in it," Monkey Breath said. "He was sliding in it."

"Actually, he was sitting *and* sliding," I pointed out.

Monkey Breath frowned and thumbed through some more pages.

"Excuse me, Principal Chump, sir," I said. "I think we're missing the big picture here. What Dusty did was part of our plan to get the key back for you."

"How?" asked Monkey Breath.

"It's kind of complicated," Wilson said.

"And we can't explain it while we're sitting in here," I added.

Monkey Breath suddenly swiveled around in his chair as if he thought someone was behind him. Then he turned back and narrowed his eyes at my friends and me.

"Do you or do you not know who has the key?" he asked.

"We think we can find out for you," I said.

"And in order to do that, you want me to let Dusty go, right?" Monkey Breath guessed.

We nodded.

Monkey Breath rubbed his chin and studied us. "You three think you're pretty smart, don't you? Well, I have news for you. I'm going to add a new rule that makes chair sliding illegal in this school. And if you three don't produce that key by the end of school today I will not only cancel the overnight trip, I will also throw the book at you!"

"Isn't throwing books against the rules?" Dusty asked.

"That's not what I meant!" Monkey Breath shouted. "Now get out!"

We were out of our seats in no time. But halfway to the door, Wilson stopped. "Uh, Principal Mon . . . I mean, Chump, sir?"

"What?" Monkey Breath yelled.

"Could I have my invention back?"

Monkey Breath tossed the glass crumb runners to him. "If I ever catch you in school with these again, you'll be sorry."

"Thanks for coming to my rescue, dudes," Dusty said, once we were out in the hall.

"No problem," said Wilson.

"No problem as long as we really have a plan, Wilson," I reminded him.

"Oh, we do," Wilson replied. "Trust me."

Wilson's plan went into motion at lunch. We waited until Cheech joined the lunch line, and a couple of kids got behind him. Then my friends and I joined the line. Cheech didn't even realize we were there.

As the line moved forward, Melody came up to us. She was in on the plan. "Dusty!" she said in a loud voice. "I read what it said about you!"

Ahead of us in the line, Cheech turned his head slightly and quickly glanced back. Then he looked forward again as if hoping we hadn't noticed he was there.

"And Kyle." Melody turned to me next. "I read what it said about *you*."

Finally, Melody turned to Wilson. "But what I really couldn't believe was what it said about *you*, Wilson."

Ahead of us, Cheech turned ever so slightly as if he needed to listen more closely.

Meanwhile, Wilson hung his head. "Was it that bad, Melody?"

"Bad?" Melody laughed loudly. "It was fantastic! I couldn't believe they were talking about Wilson Kriss! I just have one question. Are you going to Rachel's party tonight? Please say yes."

"Aw, come on, Melody," I complained.

"Sorry, Kyle," Melody said. "If you'd read what I read about Wilson, you'd be asking the same question."

"Somehow I doubt that," Dusty cracked.

Melody turned to Wilson again. "So, are you going or not?"

"Well, er . . ." Wilson hemmed and hawed.

"Please?" Melody begged him.

"Oh, give me a break!" I growled.

"You're just jealous, Kyle," Melody said. "You only wish you'd gotten a write-up like Wilson's."

"Bull," I grumbled.

"You know what?" Wilson said. "I think I will go to the party tonight."

"Gee, thanks a lot," I muttered. "Some friend."

"Oh, Wilson!" Melody threw her arms around his neck and hugged him. "I'm so glad."

Melody took off and my friends and I re-mained on the line and didn't say a thing. Ahead of us, Cheech picked up a tray and went into the kitchen.

If we were lucky, the seeds were sewn.

40

A few minutes later we sat down at our regular lunch table.

"Think he'll take the bait?" Wilson asked in a low voice.

"Do bears burp in the woods?" Dusty asked back.

"I don't know," Wilson answered. "Do they?"

"Know what's weird?" I asked. "Check out the eighth-grade table."

My friends looked over at the table where Gary Gordon and his jock friends usually hung out. It was empty.

"They're probably all at a meeting or something," Wilson said with a shrug.

"Check out Cheech." Dusty nodded toward the table where Cheech was sitting. He finished his lunch in no time, dumped his tray, and started to hurry across the cafeteria.

"Looks like he swallowed it hook, line, and sinker. He can't wait to get to the girls locker room and see what the book says." Wilson started to get up. "Come on! We have to get to the TV station."

My friends and I quickly dumped our trays and snuck out of the cafeteria.

"This is perfect," Wilson chuckled in the hall. "Just perfect! All we have to do is get Cheech on tape going into the girls locker room and — "

He stopped talking and we stopped walking. Ahead of us in the hall, a crowd of eighth-grade guys was jammed around the door to the TV studio, trying to get in.

"Come on, make room!"

"Let me see, it's my turn!"

"Yeah, don't be a hog!"

"Is this part of your plan?" Dusty asked Wilson.

Wilson shook his head slowly.

Dusty sighed. "So much for perfect."

41

Dusty joined the crowd of eighth graders and scoped out the situation. A moment later he reported back to us. "Someone figured out that there's a camera in the girls locker room."

"Did you try to explain why?" Wilson asked.

Dusty rolled his eyes. "Like they really care *why*, Wilson. All they care about is seeing girls."

"But they're not gonna see girls," Wilson said. "All they'll see is Cheech."

"They don't know that," Dusty pointed out.

"You know what's gonna happen when they see Cheech in the girls locker room?" I asked.

"They'll tell the whole school," Wilson realized.

"Everyone's gonna think Cheech is a total pervert," Dusty said.

My friends and I shared a dismal look.

"We set him up for this," I said.

"Cheech'll never live it down," said Dusty.

"It's the kind of thing that could ruin a kid's life," I said.

"If only it was Gary Gordon and not Cheech," Wilson said with a sigh.

"We should probably try to save him," I said halfheartedly.

"Cheech is all the way on the other side of the school," Dusty said. "It's probably too late."

"It's never too late!" cried Wilson.

42

Wilson yanked a chair out of a classroom. He bent down and slipped the glass crumb runners on the legs.

"It's the middle of the school day," Dusty reminded him.

"Everyone's either in class or the cafeteria," countered Wilson.

"There's a rule against chair sliding now," I pointed out. "It's on the books. If Monkey Breath catches us, we're dead."

"Cheech the Leech's reputation is on the line," said Wilson.

"Cheech the Leech doesn't *have* a reputation," Dusty said.

"Look, the only way we can get to the other side of the school fast enough to save Cheech is to use this chair," Wilson said. "Now which one of us is gonna do it?"

Dusty looked at me. I looked at Wilson.

"Kyle?" Alice was coming down the hall toward us.

"I'll do it," I said.

"You sure, Kyle?" Wilson asked.

"Kyle, I really want to talk to you," Alice said.

I grabbed the chair. "Sometimes a guy's gotta do what a guy's gotta do."

"May the Force be with you," Dusty said.

Wilson gave the runners a quick shot of silicone.

"We have to talk about the coanchor position," Alice said. "My ratings are falling."

"Later," I said as I pushed the chair past her.

Alice put her hands on her hips. "That's what you *always* say!"

It was scary how fast you could go in that chair when the glass crumb runners were greased with silicone. As I streaked down the hall, I reminded myself to tell Wilson to add a seat belt.

I turned the corner and started down the second hall. By now Cheech must have been close to the girls locker room. In fact, he may already have been *in* the girls locker room.

Would I be too late?

I turned the last corner, and started to motor. Halfway down the hall, Cheech was nearing the door to the girls locker room. Just then, farther down the hall, Monkey Breath came around the corner.

"Stop!" I yelled.

"Stop!" yelled Monkey Breath.

Cheech stopped. He saw Monkey Breath racing toward him from one end of the hall. He looked at me sliding toward him from the other end of the hall.

Then he did what any normal kid with half a brain would do.

He ran.

43

I'm still not sure who crashed into who first. But somehow, Cheech, Monkey Breath, and I wound up in a heap in the middle of the hall.

Monkey Breath sat up and held his head as if it was throbbing. "Would someone like to explain what this is all about?"

Cheech and I looked at each other and didn't say a word.

"Very well." Monkey Breath rose unsteadily to his feet. "Both of you, go to the office immediately."

Cheech and I were sitting on the office bench when Dusty and Wilson arrived.

"You got nailed?" Wilson asked.

"No, I'm sitting here for my health," I grumbled.

"Cheech, what did Monkey Breath get you for?" Dusty asked.

"Being in the hall without a pass," Cheech answered. "What's this all about anyway?"

We told him about the camera in the girls locker room.

Cheech's eyes went wide. "You mean, the whole school would have seen me?"

"That's right, dude," said Dusty.

"Wow!" Cheech slumped down on the bench and breathed a big sigh of relief.

"Dusty, keep an eye out for Monkey Breath." Wilson squatted down in front of us. "Okay, look, there's still a way for us to get out of this. But first we have to get Cheech to cooperate."

"With you guys?" Cheech snorted.

"I'm serious, Cheech," Wilson implored. "Either we work together on this or we all go down hard."

"Why should I believe you?" Cheech asked.

"Remember the other day when we surprised you in the boys' room?" I said.

Cheech nodded.

"If we'd wanted to, we could have told the whole school," said Dusty, who was standing by the window, watching for our principal.

"But we didn't tell anyone," said Wilson.

Cheech gave us a suspicious look. "Maybe you forgot."

"Maybe we decided not to because we all do dumb stuff in front of the mirror when we think no one is watching," I said.

Cheech continued to give us a suspicious look. "So what do you want me to do?"

Dusty nodded out to the hall. "He's here."

Wilson lowered his voice. "Just follow my lead."

A second later the office door swung open and Monkey Breath arrived. "What's going on?" he asked when he saw Dusty and Wilson. "What arc you two doing in here?"

"We're involved," Wilson said.

"In what?" asked our principal.

Dusty pointed at Ceech and me. "In whatever they're involved in."

Monkey Breath let out a big sigh of toxic monkey vapors. "All right, all of you go into my room."

Cheech, Dusty, Wilson, and I went into the evil Dr. Monkey Breath's dungeon and sat down. Monkey Breath peeked out of the door before closing it. Then he went to the curtains and peeked through them. Then he sat down at his desk. His right eye twitched uncontrollably.

"Have any of you seen any small green women?" he asked.

"How small?" I asked.

Principal Chump held his hand about two feet above the floor.

"I didn't think they came in that size," said Dusty.

Monkey Breath blinked and shook his head as if he were waking up from a dream. He stared across the desk at my friends and me as if he were seeing us for the first time. A crooked smile appeared on his lips. "All right. It's finally happened. I've gotten one of you on a rule that's *already* in the book. Kyle Brawly, you are charged with the crime of chair sliding."

"You know, Principal Chump," Wilson said. "Today's the day you said you'd cancel the overnight to Squeegee Lake if you didn't get the master key back."

"That's right," said Monkey Breath.

"It's a decision that the student body is going to find very unpopular," said Wilson.

"Sometimes we have to swallow bitter medicine," Monkey Breath said solemnly.

"The kids aren't going to like you for this," said Dusty.

"A principal's job is not a popularity contest," replied Monkey Breath.

"What if you could have your cake and eat it, too?" asked Wilson.

"What do you mean?" asked Monkey Breath.

"Uh . . ." Wilson fumbled. "I'm not sure. Suppose we got you the key?"

"Okay, suppose you did," Monkey Breath said.

"Wouldn't it be worth letting Kyle go?" Wilson asked.

Monkey Breath narrowed his eyes. "I get it. This is some kind of deal."

"You won't have to cancel the overnight," Wilson said.

"The whole school won't hate you," added Dusty.

"They'll probably think you're a hero for *not* canceling the overnight," I added.

Monkey Breath drummed his fingers on the desk. We could see that he was seriously thinking about it. "What about Kyle?"

"I swear I'll never do it again," I said. "I'll even organize the chair sliding police to catch anyone else who tries it."

"Cool!" Dusty said. "We could wear uniforms and hide in doorways waiting for speeders."

"We could get chair-sliding radar guns!" said Wilson.

Monkey Breath let out a big horrible toxic-smelling sigh. "All right, boys. Give me the key and I'll forget about everything."

Wilson smiled and turned to Cheech. "Okay, dude, give him the key."

Cheech frowned. "What key?"

45

My friends and I stared at Cheech in disbelief. The whole deal depended on him having the master locker room key.

"You *know* what key," Wilson sputtered. "The master key to the girls and boys locker rooms."

"What makes you think I have it?" Cheech asked.

"Of course you have it," Dusty said.

"Why would I have it?" said Cheech.

"Then how'd you write all that stuff in the kissing book?" asked Wilson.

"The what?" Monkey Breath asked.

"It's this book the girls have," Wilson explained. "They keep records of how the boys kiss."

"If the girls keep it, how could Cheech write in it?" Monkey Breath asked.

"That's our point," I said. "He couldn't write in it unless he had the key to the girls' gym lockers."

"Cheech?" Monkey Breath said.

Cheech shook his head. "I've heard of that book, but why would I want to write in it?"

"To make yourself look good and the rest of us look bad," I said.

Cheech just shrugged.

"Look," Wilson said to Monkey Breath, "everything we've told you is true. And if you don't believe us, you can ask Ms. Fortune. Not only does she know about the kissing book, she actually *has* it."

Monkey Breath pushed the intercom button on his phone. "Ms. Fortune, would you come in here, please?"

A moment later Ms. Fortune came in.

"Have you ever heard of something called the kissing book?" Monkey Breath asked.

Ms. Fortune frowned.

Then she looked at us.

Then she said, "No."

My friends and I were shocked. Then I remembered the deal we'd made. If we promised to be really good, Ms. Fortune had promised not to tell Monkey Breath about the kissing book. She was just keeping her promise!

Monkey Breath's face turned dark red. His eyes narrowed into slits. "Thank you, Ms. Fortune. You may go."

Ms. Fortune left. Monkey Breath picked up a

Styrofoam coffee cup and slowly crushed it in his fist. "Trying to make a fool of me, huh?"

"But — " Wilson started to say.

"No buts!" Monkey Breath screamed. My friends and I were sprayed with little droplets of highly toxic monkey spit.

"I've had it with you!" he yelled. "No more deals! No more lies! You're all going to be suspended!"

"Even me?" Cheech asked.

"No, not you," Monkey Breath said. "You can go."

Cheech stood up and turned to my friends and me. "Sorry, guys. Guess I'll see you when your suspension's over."

46

Free to go, Cheech headed for the dungeon door.

For the rest of us, it was like a nightmare.

My friends and I were telling the truth, but Monkey Breath was convinced we were lying.

Cheech had to be lying, but Monkey Breath was convinced he was telling the truth!

And now we were all going to be suspended!

"We've been scammed by Cheech," Dusty groaned.

He was right. Cheech had only *pretended* to go along with our plan. We'd been double-crossed!

Cheech reached the door and started to pull it open. Then he stopped and turned to Monkey Breath. "Principal Chump?"

"Yes?" answered Monkey Breath.

"You'd really suspend these guys?" Cheech asked.

"Absolutely," our principal replied.

"Because you think they lied to you about the kissing book and the key?"

"That's correct," said Monkey Breath.

Cheech looked at my friends and me. "You know, you guys have given me a lot of grief. I mean, for *years*."

My friends and I glanced at each other. None of us knew what to say. We *had* given Cheech a lot of grief.

"I know you guys thought it was all just for fun," Cheech went on. "But sometimes even 'just for fun' isn't so funny to the guy it's happening to."

We nodded. We could see that now.

"The thing is," Cheech went on, "twice when you had the chance to do something *really* mean, you didn't do it. I guess that means that deep down you're okay dudes."

My friends and I shrugged. It was nice to hear Cheech say that, but it wasn't exactly going to do any of us much good now.

Then Cheech dug into his pocket and tossed something onto Monkey Breath's desk. "There's your key, Principal Chump."

Monkey Breath's mouth fell open. "How?"

"Found it," Cheech said. "And you said that if you got it, you'd forget about everything."

"Yes, but — " Monkey Breath began.

"No buts," Cheech said with a grin.

A few moments later Dusty, Wilson, Cheech, and I were walking down the hall. We were free and out of trouble. The kissing book was in Ms. Fortune's office where no one could read it or write in it again. The annual school trip to Squeegee Lake would go on as planned.

"I have to hand it to you, Cheech," Dusty said. "You really got us back good."

"Better than good," Wilson stressed.

"Thanks, dudes." Cheech grinned. "No hard feelings?"

"Nah." We shook our heads. "We got you, you got us. We're even."

"So what do you want to do tonight?" Cheech asked.

My friends and I stopped and shared a look.

"Go to the spin the bottle party, what else?" Dusty said.

"Great idea!" agreed Wilson.

"Yeah, I can't wait to make some of those girls change their opinions," I said.

Cheech's jaw dropped and he looked pale. "Are you serious?"

My friends and I all grinned. "No!"

48

Hey, this is Dusty Lane, Kyle's friend. In the last DON'T GET CAUGHT book Wilson got to tell you some cool stuff to do. And in the book before that, Kyle had some good pointers. Now it's my turn.

I've got an idea I think you'll like. But first, Todd Strasser asked me to warn you not to try chair sliding at your school. Here's the reason. Pretend a kid sliding in a chair is a bowling ball. Next, pretend the hall is a bowling alley. Finally, pretend the kids and teachers at the far end of the hall are bowling pins.

Get the idea?

All you have to do is roll a strike and some-one's gonna get hurt.

Instead, here's something you can do to show the strongest kid you know that your index fingers are stronger than his arms.

Have him make fists and put one fist on top of the other as if he were holding a baseball bat.

Next, have him stretch his arms straight out, keeping his fists in the same position.

Now stick out the index finger on each of your hands. Hit the back of his right fist with your left index finger and at the same time the back of his left fist with your right. There's no way he'll be able to keep his fists together. Your fingers are stronger than his arms. You must be one tough dude, dude.

About the Author

Todd Strasser has written many award-winning novels for young and teenage readers. Among his best-known books are *Help! I'm Trapped in Obedience School* and *Help! I'm Trapped in Santa's Body.* His most recent books for Scholastic are *Help! I'm Trapped in My Lunch Lady's Body* and *Help! I'm Trapped in a Professional Wrestler's Body.*

The movie *Next to You,* starring Melissa Joan Hart, was based on his novel *How I Created My Perfect Prom Date.*

Todd speaks frequently at schools about the craft of writing and conducts writing workshops for young people. He and his family live outside New York City with their yellow Labrador retriever, Mac.

You can find out more about Todd and his books at http://www.toddstrasser.com